THE *Princess* IN **BLACK**
and the MYSTERIOUS PLAYDATE

THE *Princess* IN
BLACK
and the MYSTERIOUS PLAYDATE

Shannon Hale & Dean Hale

illustrated by
LeUyen Pham

CANDLEWICK PRESS

Text copyright © 2017 by Shannon and Dean Hale
Illustrations copyright © 2017 by LeUyen Pham

First edition 2017

Library of Congress Catalog Card Number pending
ISBN 978-0-7636-8826-4

17 18 19 20 21 22 LEO 10 9 8 7 6 5 4 3 2 1

Printed in Heshan, Guangdong, China

This book was typeset in LTC Kennerley Pro.
The illustrations were done in watercolor and ink.

Candlewick Press
99 Dover Street
Somerville, Massachusetts 02144

visit us at www.candlewick.com

Chapter 1

It was a clear, crisp, comfortable afternoon. The Princess in Black and the Goat Avenger had just sent a monster back into the hole. The hole led to Monster Land. It was time for the victory dance.

They slapped hands. They wiggled bums. They said "Calloo!" It was their thing.

Neither of them noticed a new monster sneaking out of the hole.

"Can you guard the goats for the rest of the day?" asked the Princess in Black. "I have . . . plans. Mysterious plans."

"Mysterious plans are the best kind," said the Goat Avenger.

They did the victory dance again. Just because.

The Princess in Black turned to leave. The sneaky monster quickly squatted into the shape of a bush.

"Was that bush always there?" asked the Princess in Black.

But the Goat Avenger didn't hear.
He was busy practicing ninja moves.
He said "Ya!" and "Look out!" and
"Hup-whup-woo!"

The Princess in Black and Blacky galloped through the forest. They stopped when they reached Princess Magnolia's castle.

Now they had to be careful. If anyone saw the Princess in Black going into the castle, they might figure out that she was Princess Magnolia. And no one knew the Princess in Black's secret identity. Except Blacky, of course.

The Princess in Black looked right. Blacky looked left. The coast was clear.

The pony dived into the secret passage. The princess jumped the castle wall.

They were certain no one had seen them.

Chapter 2

The sneaky monster crept toward the castle drawbridge. It was hungry. All it wanted was to eat goats. The Princess in Black smelled like goats. So the sneaky monster had followed her.

Now she had disappeared. So the sneaky monster squatted into the shape of a stone. And it waited.

Soon a unicorn came across the drawbridge. It was pulling a buggy.

A princess sat in the buggy. She was wearing pink. She couldn't possibly be the Princess in Black. But she did smell like goats.

"Eat goats . . ." the monster whispered.

A masked hero was protecting the goats back at the goat pasture. The sneaky monster would follow this princess. She didn't look like trouble. And she would surely lead it to some goats. Though any smelly, shaggy creatures would do.

Chapter 3

Frimplepants pulled the buggy around a mountain. Soon Princess Magnolia could smell the salty sea air.

"We're here, Frimplepants!" said Princess Magnolia. "Princess Sneezewort's kingdom!"

The trolley cars were clacking.
The surf was rolling. What a perfect
day for mysterious plans. Plans like a
princess playdate!

Princess Sneezewort's castle was
in the center of town.

Princess Magnolia knocked on the front door.

"Princess Sneezewort, I'm here for our princess playdate!" said Princess Magnolia.

No one came to the door.

"Princess Sneezewort?" Princess Magnolia called out. "Anybody home?"

Princess Sneezewort cleared her throat. "I'm right here beside you," she said.

"Oh!" said Princess Magnolia. "I didn't notice. You blend in so well with the flowers."

Princess Sneezewort's pig, Sir Hogswell, showed Frimplepants the garden. Princess Sneezewort showed Princess Magnolia the castle.

"This is the throne room," said Princess Sneezewort. "But I misplaced the throne."

"It happens," said Princess Magnolia.

"This is the ballroom," said Princess Sneezewort. "It's where I keep the balls."

"Very practical," said Princess Magnolia.

"This is the playroom," said Princess Sneezewort. "I think there are other rooms in the castle, but I'm usually here."

"Shall we?" said Princess Magnolia. "After you," said Princess Sneezewort.

Princess Magnolia and Princess Sneezewort waged playdate.

DRESS-UP SLAM!

PLAYTIME ROMP!

KARAOKE JAM! ✽

SNACK-TIME STOMP! ✽

Princess Magnolia was having an excellent time. She was so far away from home that her monster alarm didn't even work. So surely no monster attack would interrupt the fun.

Chapter 4

A shout from outside interrupted the fun. It came from the park across the street.

"Help! Help! A monster is trying to eat my kitty!"

"A monster? Noseholes and elephants!" exclaimed Princess Sneezewort.

"Oh, dear!" said Princess Magnolia.

"You stay here," said Princess
Sneezewort. "I'll go see what's
wrong."

Princess Sneezewort was certain that prim and perfect Princess Magnolia was afraid of monsters. After all, she was afraid of snails. She was afraid of getting her face wet. Earthworms made her woozy.

So Princess Sneezewort smiled kindly. She shut the playroom door softly. And then she ran.

Princess Sneezewort felt uncertain. Should Princess Sneezewort protect her kingdom? Certainly! But did she know how? No . . . no, she didn't.

Luckily she had read about the Princess in Black in *Princess* magazine.

HOW TO BE A MONSTER-BATTLING HERO

Step 1: Wear a disguise.

No one knew the Princess in Black's secret identity. Princess Sneezewort supposed she must hide hers too. She ducked into the linen closet. She looked around. What to wear for a disguise?

Chapter 5

As soon as the coast was clear, Princess Magnolia ran too. She jumped out the window and into a shrub. Off with her princess clothes. On with her mask. Out of the shrub, across the street, and into the park.

"The princess is back!" said the Princess in Black.

But she couldn't see any monsters in the park. Only a crying girl, a shaky kitty, and a masked stranger.

"Who are you?" asked the Princess in Black.

"Me?" said the masked stranger. "Well, I am most definitely . . . uh . . . the Princess in Blankets!"

The Princess in Blankets posed with her fists on her hips. A corner of a blanket flopped over her eyes. She pushed it out of the way.

"Excellent!" said the Princess in Black. "I could use some help. Let's save the day!"

They comforted the little girl.
They petted the kitty.

They examined monster footprints.
But the monster was nowhere to be seen.

Chapter 6

The Princess in Blankets sneaked back into the castle. She hid from the servants. She crept into the linen closet. Then she strolled into the playroom.

"I'm back!" said Princess Sneezewort.

Princess Magnolia was reading a book. Her cheeks were pink, as if she'd been running. But that was silly. Princesses do not run.

"What happened?" asked Princess Magnolia.

"A monster sneaked into the park," said Princess Sneezewort. "It tried to eat a kitty. Then the Princess in Black showed up."

"What a surprise!" said Princess Magnolia. "Did she stop the monster?"

"It disappeared. Um, there was a new hero too. The Princess in Blankets."

"Well," said Princess Magnolia. "Two heroes will certainly take care of one monster."

"Yes," said Princess Sneezewort. "We can leave it to them."

"Help!" came a shout from outside.
"Monster!"

The princesses looked at each other.

"I need to go . . . uh, to the bathroom," Princess Magnolia muttered.
"Is it down the hall?" She started for a door.

"Yes, that way," Princess Sneezewort mumbled. "I should look for the
misplaced throne. . . ." She started
for the other door.

As soon as she was alone, Princess
Sneezewort ran.

HOW TO BE A
MONSTER-BATTLING HERO

Step 1: Wear a disguise.
Step 2: Ride a brave, masked beast.

It took some blankets, twine, and a carrot. Now Sir Hogswell was the fearsome unicorn hero, Corny!

The Princess in Blankets rode Corny into the park. She lifted her fist into the air.

"The princess is blanketed!" said the Princess in Blankets. "Look out, monsters!"

But there was no monster. Just a little boy, his shaggy dog, and the Princess in Black.

"A monster tried to eat my puppy!" the little boy said. "But when you came, it disappeared."

"Udders and moo cows!" said the Princess in Blankets. "We must find that monster!"

The Princess in Black rode Blacky around the park.

The Princess in Blankets rode Corny. Mostly around in circles. Corny did not believe in great distances.

One hero searched far. The other
hero searched near. But they couldn't
find the monster.

Chapter 7

I won't rest until I find that monster!" said the Princess in Black.

Blacky reared. He neighed a mighty neigh. They rode off to search the city.

"Me too!" said the Princess in Blankets.

She leaped onto Corny's back.
Corny curled up. He snored a mighty
snore.

ZZZZ

The Princess in Blankets hoped
that Princess Magnolia was taking
her time in the bathroom. Because
this monster-hunting business was
about as speedy as Corny.

The Princess in Blankets tapped her chin. The monster kept trying to eat pets in this very park. It must be hiding nearby. She would find it! She would save the day!

HOW TO BE A MONSTER-BATTLING HERO
Step 1: Wear a disguise.
Step 2: Ride a brave, masked beast.
Step 3: Do lots of cool ninja moves.

The Princess in Blankets kicked a bush. Her shoe fell off. She put it back on.

The Princess in Blankets punched a tree. She got a scratch. She put on a bandage.

The Princess in Blankets did a fear-some twirl. She got dizzy. She had to sit down.

"What are you doing?" asked a boy who was walking his pet llama.

"Battling a monster," said the Princess in Blankets.

"Doesn't look like it," said the boy. The llama blew air out of its lips. It seemed to agree.

The Princess in Blankets sniffled. She chin-quivered. She thought about crying. She felt uncertain about being a hero. She didn't have ninja skills. Not like the Princess in Black.

"Wow," said the boy. "When you sit still, I almost can't see you. Pretty sneaky."

The Princess in Blankets remembered something she had read in *Ninja* magazine.

NINJA SKILLS
1. Cool battle moves
2. Good at climbing
3. Pretty sneaky

Perhaps she had a ninja skill after all. The Princess in Blankets nestled between some trees. She held so still, not even Corny knew she was there. And then she waited.

Chapter 8

The sneaky monster was hungry. There were no goats in this park. Only shaggy, non-goat pets. They smelled yummy. But every time the sneaky monster tried to taste one, a hero showed up.

So the sneaky monster had to pretend to be a park bench. Being bench-shaped was uncomfortable. Plus sometimes people sat on you.

A pet was curled up and sleeping in the park. It was not a goat. But it smelled delicious.

The sneaky monster looked left. It looked right.

The coast was clear.

The sneaky monster unfolded out of its bench shape. It crept toward the snoozy, non-goat pet.

"How very curious," said a voice.

There was a flapping of blankets. Suddenly, a hero appeared. The monster squeaked in surprise. But then it snarled.

"EAT PETS!" the monster said.

"You may not eat the pets," said the Princess in Blankets.

This hero did not look dangerous. And it was shaggy. Maybe it was yummy.

"EAT YOU?" the monster said.

The sneaky monster pounced. The Princess in Blankets tried to run. The monster got tangled in one of her blankets. It tore the blanket loose. It roared.

The sneaky monster looked like it was playing dress-up. And that gave the Princess in Blankets an idea.

She took the karaoke microphone out of her pocket. She shouted into it.

"Oh, Princess in Black! Do you want to have a hero princess play-date?"

In the distance, a pony neighed.

Chapter 9

The Princess in Black galloped back into the park. The Princess in Blankets was throwing extra blankets over a monster. It tried to sneak away. But it was too blankety to sneak.

"Dress-up Slam!" said the Princess in Blankets.

The Princess in Black nodded. And then the two heroes waged playdate.

PLAYTIME ROMP! ❀

KARAOKE JAM! ❀

SNACK-TIME STOMP!

UNICORN RAM!

The sneaky monster didn't look so sneaky anymore. It looked dizzy.

"EAT PETS?" growled the dizzy monster.

"Behave, beast!" said the two heroes.

"I'm taking you back to Monster
Land!" said the Princess in Black.
"Care to join me, Princess in Blankets?
Um, where are you?"

"Right here. I thought you could
use this extra twine."

"Wow," said the Princess in Black, "you have great ninja skills. I didn't even see you there."

The Princess in Blankets smiled. Together, they hog-tied the monster.

Chapter 10

The Goat Avenger had just sent a monster back to Monster Land. He was sweating. He was grinning. He was wishing there were someone to join in his victory dance. Besides the goats.

Just then the Princess in Black and
Blacky galloped into the goat pasture.

"We have a monster to return to
Monster Land," the Princess in Black
announced.

"We?" asked the Goat Avenger.

"Yes!" said the Princess in Black.
"Let me introduce . . . the Princess in
Blankets!"

"Hello!" said the new hero. She ambled into the pasture on the back of a roundish unicorn.

"We're having a hero princess playdate," said the Princess in Black. "Would you like to join us?"

The Goat Avenger felt uncertain. He wanted to play. But he did not think he was a princess.

"What do you do on a hero princess playdate?" asked the Goat Avenger.

"Battle monsters," said the Princess in Black. "Also, eat snacks."

"And dance and sing," added the Princess in Blankets. "But mostly battle monsters."

The Goat Avenger smiled. A hero princess playdate sounded like an excellent idea.

First they sent the sneaky monster
back to Monster Land.

Then it was time for the victory dance.
The three heroes slapped hands. They
wiggled bums. They said "Calloo!"
It was their thing.